HOW TO WRITE A BESTSELLING WORKPLACE ROMANCE

FROM CUBICLE CRUSHES TO PUBLISHING SUCCESS

JUST BAE

CONTENTS

1

UNVEILING THE DYNAMICS OF WORKPLACE ROMANCE

Introduction to the Genre

Workplace romance novels have established a unique space within the vast romance genre, enchanting readers with their depiction of love flourishing amid the intricacies of professional environments. The narratives center on characters who skillfully maneuver through the delicate balance of professional aspirations and romantic entanglements. Placing romance in the workplace setting, these stories deliver a captivating mix of emotional richness and professional excitement.

In workplace romance stories, the office becomes a vibrant backdrop where characters engage, confront obstacles, and ultimately discover love. The setting serves not just as a backdrop, but as a dynamic force that influences the narrative and character interactions. The workplace setting, be it a vibrant corporate office, a quaint bakery in a small town, or a busy hospital ward, is essential in propelling the narrative ahead.

Workplace romance novels captivate readers for a variety of compelling reasons. This sub-genre delivers an engaging blend of everyday situations and imaginative escapism, striking a perfect harmony between the known and the surprising. This narrative weaves together the fabric of daily existence with the captivating thrill of unexpected romance, generating a magnetic tension that compels readers to keep turning the pages.

Workplace romances captivate by connecting with readers' own experiences, offering a thrilling escape into a world filled with love and ambition. The dynamics of the workplace introduce intricate challenges and heightened tension to romantic relationships, compelling characters to skillfully maneuver between their personal aspirations and professional obligations. Power struggles, ethical dilemmas, and office politics create challenges that characters must navigate in their quest for love, enriching the narrative with depth and intrigue.

Additionally, novels centered around workplace romance provide a distinctive chance to delve into themes that are particular to this sub-genre. Crafting a captivating workplace romance story demands a keen insight into the essential components and common motifs that strike a chord with audiences. By weaving these elements into their story-telling, authors can craft engaging narratives that enthrall readers from diverse backgrounds and tastes.

In the upcoming chapters, we will explore the intricate elements of crafting a captivating workplace romance novel that captures readers' hearts. We will delve into the vital techniques and insights from bestselling authors in the genre, covering everything from structuring the narrative and crafting captivating dialogue to navigating workplace dynamics and weaving in humor. By grasping the allure of workplace romances and the desires of their audience, aspiring authors can set out on a journey to craft captivating narratives that keep readers coming back for more.

The Appeal of Workplace Romance

Readers of workplace romance books find themselves drawn to them because of their unusual mix of escapist fantasy and relevant situations. These tales transport readers into a world where the lines separating personal needs from work obligations blur and provide a seductive mix of daily living and unannounced love.

The dynamic environment in which workplace romances develop is one of the main reasons they appeal so much. Characters meet problems, engage, and finally discover romance on the stage that is the workplace. It shapes the tale and influences character dynamics, thereby acting not just as a background but also as an active participant. From a busy corporate office to a small-town bakery to a high-stress hospital, the employment environment gives the love relationships shown in these books levels of complexity and stress.

Characters in the workplace have to negotiate a careful mix between their job responsibilities and their love goals. Readers are kept interested by the intriguing conflict this interaction between love and ambition generates. The obstacles and sacrifices characters must make in order to follow their love desires while balancing the responsibilities of their professions capt appeal them. The conflicts that surface—power battles, moral conundrums, workplace politics—bring complexity to the narrative and provide chances for personal development.

Furthermore, workplace romance books let readers investigate the forbidden or surprising sides of love. Unquestionably, the appeal of romance flowering in the workplace is great. It offers a feeling of vicarious exhilaration and escape in addition to appealing to the fundamental human need for connection and company. Readers become engross in the protagonists' travels and eagerly flip the pages to see how they negotiate the complexity of their professional relationships.

Knowing the attraction of professional relationships helps writers create stories that appeal to readers from all backgrounds and tastes. Age, occupation, and life events—

among other demographic factors—can guide the narrative and assist in the development of characters and scenarios readers can identify with. Workplace romance books have the ability to move readers to tears and carry them into a world where love and ambition intersect, whether that means a young intern falling in love with a seasoned CEO or two coworkers overcoming their professional rivalry.

The following part will look at the main ideas and components that give workplace romance books such appeal. We will explore the well chosen office environments that transcend simple background scenes, the professional tensions that deepen the narrative, and the core subject of romantic tension guiding the emotional path of the book. Knowing these components can help ambitious writers start to create their own workplace romance stories that enthrall readers and make a lasting impact.

Key Elements and Themes

Several main components and recurrent themes that help to explain their popularity and success define workplace romance books. Knowing and using these components and themes into your work will enable you to write a gripping workplace romance novel that appeals to readers.

The well constructed office environment is a must component of workplace romance books. The workplace should actively construct the story and impact the relationships among people, not just provide a background. Whether it's a small-town bakery, a corporate office, or a high-stress hospital, the workplace should be realistically shown so that readers could really enter the world of the people. Capturing the core of the workplace can help you to provide a rich and real background for your relationship to develop.

Another very vital component in workplace romance books are professional disputes. By posing challenges that people must overcome to follow their love desires, power battles, moral conundrums, and workplace politics provide the narrative complexity. These disputes keep readers interested by generating suspense and tension, therefore guiding the story along. Including reasonable working problems can help you to give your relationship additional levels of depth, therefore increasing its appeal and relatability.

Workplace romance books revolve mostly on romantic conflict. It keeps readers engaged in the tale and drives the emotional arc of it. The fragile equilibrium created by the main characters' wants, professional obligations, and push and pull feeds the romantic suspense. From a forbidden workplace romance to a love-hate relationship between coworkers to a hidden affair, the unresolved emotions and desire between the characters should be evident all through the story. Readers will be fervently flipping the pages, anxious to know how the love tale turns out, if you deftly create and sustain romantic suspense.

Understanding the expectations of the target audience and including demographic issues into your narrative can help you to produce a workplace romance book appealing to a broad spectrum of readers. diverse readers have diverse tastes and backgrounds hence it's crucial to blend universal topics with particular subtleties. Researching extensively and knowing the demographics of your target audience can help you create real and relevant stories and characters. This meticulous attention to detail will help the readers to relate to the story and raise the general attraction of your workplace romance book.

Key components and topics in office romance books are therefore the well chosen working environment, professional tensions, romantic tension, and demographic concerns. By deftly combining these components into your writing, you may create a gripping office romance novel that hooks readers in a world where ambition and love meet.

2

———

CRAFTING A COMPELLING NARRATIVE WITH A THREE-ACT FRAMEWORK

Understanding the Three-Act Structure in a Workplace Romance Context

In storytelling, the three-act structure has stood the test of time as a reliable framework for crafting engaging narratives. This structure becomes a powerful tool for creating a compelling and satisfying story when applied to workplace romance novels. Understanding the three acts - Setup, Confrontation, and Resolution - is crucial for aspiring authors looking to write a bestselling workplace romance.

The *setup* is where the foundation of the story is laid. In this initial act, authors introduce the workplace environment and the main characters, setting the stage for the romantic tension to unfold. It is in the Setup that readers become acquainted with the unique dynamics of the workplace and the initial interactions between the protagonists. By immersing readers in this world, authors can establish the stakes and the potential for romance to blossom.

Moving into the *confrontation*, the plot gains momentum as obstacles and conflicts arise. These challenges can come from both romantic and professional spheres, testing the protagonists' ability to navigate the complexities of their relationship while also fulfilling their professional duties. It is during this act that the tension between the characters reaches its peak, as they grapple with their feelings for each other while facing external pressures that threaten to tear them apart.

Finally, the *resolution* brings the story to a satisfying conclusion. In this third act, authors tie up loose ends, resolve conflicts, and deliver a resolution that leaves readers feeling fulfilled. It is crucial to strike a balance between providing closure for the romantic relationship and addressing any lingering professional conflicts. By doing so, authors can create an emotionally resonant ending that leaves readers with a sense of satisfaction and closure.

To illustrate the power of the three-act structure in a workplace romance context, let's consider an example. Imagine a workplace romance novel set in a bustling advertising agency. In the Setup, the author introduces the workplace environment, showcasing the fast-paced nature of the industry and the unique dynamics between the employees. The main characters, a talented copywriter and a charismatic art director, meet for the first time, sparking an immediate connection.

As the story progresses into the confrontation, the protagonists face numerous obstacles that test their budding romance. They find themselves competing for the same promotion, leading to professional tensions that spill over into their personal lives. Additionally, a client's unexpected demands put their working relationship to the test, forcing them to navigate the delicate balance between their professional responsibilities and their growing feelings for each other.

Finally, in the resolution, the protagonists overcome their conflicts and find a way to reconcile their personal and professional lives. They collaborate on a groundbreaking advertising campaign that not only secures the promotion they both desired but also strengthens their bond. The novel concludes with a heartfelt declaration of love and a glimpse into their future as a successful power couple in the advertising industry.

By adhering to the three-act structure, authors can effectively guide readers through the ups and downs of a workplace romance, ensuring a well-paced and emotionally satisfying journey. The Setup establishes the foundation, the Confrontation builds tension, and the Resolution delivers a resolution that leaves readers longing for more. With this understanding, authors can confidently embark on crafting a workplace romance novel that captivates readers and has the potential to become a bestseller.

Identifying Major Plot Points and Turning Points

Crafting a compelling workplace romance novel requires effectively identifying and utilizing major plot points and turning points. These pivotal moments shape the story's direction and keep readers engaged and invested in the protagonists' journey. By understanding the significance of these narrative elements, authors can create a dynamic and captivating workplace romance narrative.

Major plot points are key moments in the story that have a significant impact on the overall plot. These moments serve as milestones that drive the narrative forward and heighten the stakes for the protagonists. For instance, the initial meeting of the protagonists can be a major plot point that sparks the romantic tension and sets the stage for their developing relationship. This moment allows readers to witness the initial chemistry and connection between the characters, creating anticipation for what lies ahead.

Another major plot point in a workplace romance novel could be a significant conflict arising in the workplace. This conflict could result from office politics, a promotion opportunity, or a clash of professional goals. By introducing such conflicts, authors can add depth and complexity to the story, highlighting the challenges the protagonists face in balancing their personal and professional lives.

Furthermore, a romantic revelation can serve as a major plot point that propels the story forward. This revelation can be a character admitting their feelings for the other protagonist or a realization of true love. This moment not only intensifies the romantic tension but also creates a turning point in the narrative, leading to new conflicts and challenges for the protagonists to overcome.

Turning points, on the other hand, are moments of change within the story that propel the narrative forward. These moments can be unexpected events, decisions, or realizations that have a profound impact on the protagonists and their relationship. For example, a betrayal by a colleague or a workplace incident that tests the protagonists' bond can serve as a turning point. These moments create tension and raise the stakes, pushing the protagonists to confront their feelings and make important choices that shape the course of the story.

By identifying and effectively utilizing major plot points and turning points, authors can create a compelling workplace romance narrative that keeps readers hooked. These moments of significance not only provide opportunities for character development but also allow for the exploration of complex emotions and conflicts. The careful placement and execution of these narrative elements ensure a well-paced and engaging storyline that captivates readers from beginning to end.

Balancing Romance and Professional Conflicts Seamlessly

Striking a careful balance between the emotional and professional issues that develop within an office romance book is really essential. Authors may create a story that is both realistic and interesting to readers by deftly combining these two elements. This part will look at methods and approaches for striking this balance so that your workplace romance book will appeal to its target market.

Interweaving your heroes' personal and professional life can help you to strike a good balance between romance and career challenges. Showing how their love affects their employment and vice versa can help you to build a multi-dimensional narrative exploring the complexity of professional romance. You may demonstrate, for instance, how a promotion or a transfer changes the dynamics between the heroes or how a working disagreement permeates their home life and tests their partnership.

Another approach is to design conflicts arising especially from the dynamics of your characters in the workplace. To provide complexity and suspense, think about including power relationships, workplace politics, and competitiveness into your narrative. You may discuss the difficulties maintaining a professional image while negotiating a developing relationship or bring in a competitive colleague who also becomes a love competitor. These workplace disputes may provide chances to investigate the complexity of balancing professional obligations with personal aspirations as well as spur on character development.

Moreover, showing how the connection of the heroes affects their professions can provide your story even more complexity. Emphasizing the ways in which their love engagement influences their career choices, goals, and objectives helps one to reach this. You may investigate, for instance, the inner conflict of a character caught between following a promotion and keeping a hidden connection or the difficulties preserving a professional reputation while working with a colleague. Combining the personal and professional aspects of your characters' life can help you to produce a rich and complex narrative that appeals to readers.

Consider a workplace romance story set in a high-powered corporate atmosphere to show the perfect mix of passion and professional tensions. James and Sarah, the heroes, are driven professionals aiming for success in their different fields. They get caught in a web of office politics and power battles as they negotiate their increasing attraction to one another. James struggles with the moral ramifications of pursuing a relationship with a subordinate; Sarah is caught between her affection for James and her need to be taken seriously as a leader in her profession. Examining the issues resulting from their workplace dynamics and the effects of their relationship on their professional life helps the narrative explore the difficulties and complexity of juggling romance and job goals.

Readers will be captivated by a workplace romance tale that deftly combines love tension with business strife. Keep in mind the entwining of personal and professional life, including problems resulting from workplace dynamics, and highlight how the connection of the heroes influences their professions. These methods will help your tale come alive with realism and appeal to people looking for a gripping workplace romance novel.

3

CREATING A PRODUCTIVE
WORKPLACE ENVIRONMENT

Choosing the Right Workplace Setting

The environment you choose for your workplace romance book will have a significant impact on the characters' interactions and dynamics. Love may blossom in any office setting, but it comes with its own set of advantages and disadvantages. Picking the correct office environment is a great way to add mystery and depth to your story.

You should think about the different kinds of workplaces and how they might affect the plot of your novel. For instance, power battles and hierarchical connections may be seen in a business workplace. Anxieties and complexity in the love plot might be brought to light by competing goals and the challenges of managing the working world. Conversely, working in a small company allows for a more personal and tight-knit atmosphere, perfect for the kind of relationship-building that flourishes when people work together for common objectives.

Create an interesting tale by highlighting the differences between various employment contexts. For example, characters' love tensions and emotions are heightened at hospitals because of the high-stakes circumstances that take place there. A feeling of vulnerability and urgency brought on by the work's potential life-or-death implications might enrich the relationship. Conversely, there are plenty of possibilities for your characters to bond in unexpected places, like a creative agency or a busy cafe.

Think about the unique dynamics and connections that could develop in each work environment to make a well-informed choice. Cast your mind back to the characters' jobs and how those obligations shape their relationships and interactions with coworkers. You may provide a vibrant background that supports the characters' emotional journey by meticulously selecting the correct workplace.

Consider a legal firm. The industry's cutthroat nature may lead to a heated environment where individuals are always in conflict with one another. Intense arguments and passionate encounters might ensue, propelling the relationship forward. On the other hand, a tumultuous newsroom might provide an exciting setting where people are always racing against the clock, which could lead to a bonding experience fueled by a shared adrenaline rush.

Your story will be more realistic and interesting to readers if you take into account the specific dynamics of various workplaces. In addition to setting the scene for the relationship, your characters' work environment should provoke development, emotional connection, and conflict. If you're writing a romance story set in a workplace, make sure the location is important.

4

CREATING SPARKS: BUILDING ROMANTIC TENSION

Creating Chemistry Between Characters

Focusing on how characters interact, respond, and feel is important for creating a real and interesting link between them. You can help readers care about the connection and feel the chemistry between the characters by focusing on things like shared hobbies, traits that suit each other, and real times of weakness.

Deep conversations are a good way to get to know each other better. Plan talks that bring out the energy and attraction that are already there. For instance, in a romance at work, have the characters joke around or tease each other in a way that hints at their shared interest. You can make the characters feel like they have a strong connection by using conversation to show secret feelings and subtext.

Conversations and body language aren't the only ways to build chemistry. Showing the characters' body language, like eager looks, light touches, or worried fidgeting, can give their relationships more depth and make you want more. These nonverbal cues can show what people want without them saying it, which can make the love drama between the characters stronger.

Also, looking into the characters' inner journeys can make the chemistry between them stronger in a working romance. Let the readers see their weaknesses and fears, as well as how they change as the story goes on. To make a strong bond that readers can relate to, show how the characters help and understand each other on an emotional level.

One character might tell the other about their fears or tell a personal story that shows who they really are. This openness can help the characters feel connected to each other deeply, which can make their relationship more real and interesting.

Overall, getting people in an office romance to connect through conversation, body language, and emotional depth is a tricky business. Write conversations between your characters that show how attracted they are to each other, how vulnerable they are, and how you want their relationship to grow naturally. This will help you build a strong base for an interesting story that readers will want to see succeed.

Developing Slow-Burn Romance

One of the most captivating aspects of office romance is the slow-burn, the way a profound relationship develops over time, which engrosses and engages readers. In this investigation, we will learn the ins and outs of crafting a slow-burn romance, which lays the groundwork for a fulfilling love story by letting the relationship grow organically over time.

Building suspense and desire between the characters is key to writing an engaging slow-burn romance. Incorporating scenes of yearning, lost chances, and understated gestures that suggest an underlying desire might help accomplish this. To keep readers interested in the slow-burn romance and increase the suspense, think about using the following strategies.

Building Emotional Connections: Emotional depth is the lifeblood of slow-burn romances. As the characters traverse the complexities of the workplace, let their emotions evolve and intensify over time. Highlighting vulnerability, shared experiences, and authentic moments of connection can create a powerful emotional bond between the characters. Explore their fears, dreams, and aspirations to build a solid foundation of trust and understanding that ignites their blossoming attraction.

In a corporate environment, the male lead might possess a complicated history that has influenced his reserved demeanor. The female protagonist is driven and ambitious, yet she grapples with a deep-seated fear of vulnerability.

Amidst the pressures of a high-stakes project, their shared experiences and moments of vulnerability gradually dismantle their emotional walls, creating an opportunity for a profound connection to flourish.

Encouraging Delicate Actions: In a gradual romance, it's the subtle details that truly convey deep meaning. Delicate movements can express hidden emotions and intensify the allure of romance. Infuse your narrative with subtle gestures of kindness, fleeting glances, or unintentional touches that ignite a deep longing within the characters. These moments evoke a deep sense of yearning and excitement, compelling readers to keep flipping through the pages.

During a team-building retreat, the two main characters are paired up for a trust exercise. As they maneuver through the obstacle course, the male protagonist deftly directs the female protagonist, his touch lingering just a heartbeat longer than required. A brief encounter ignites a spark of interest, paving the way for a simmering romance to develop over time.

Uncovering Overlooked Possibilities: Missed opportunities serve as compelling catalysts in a slow-burn romance, heightening the desire that simmers between the characters. Imagine scenarios where the characters find themselves unable to reveal their genuine emotions or make progress in their relationship. Missed opportunities generate tension and amplify the longing for resolution.

Picture this: the two protagonists are teetering on the edge of revealing their true feelings in the midst of a late-night work session. Yet, an unforeseen interruption or a call from a loved one abruptly halts the moment, leaving both characters longing for the opportunity to share their feelings.

Incorporating these techniques allows you to craft a slow-burn romance that steadily develops emotional connections, nurtures subtle gestures, and delves into missed opportunities. As the characters maneuver through the intricacies of the workplace, their escalating attraction will leave readers on the edge of their seats, eagerly awaiting the moment when their love bursts into flames.

Using Obstacles Strategically

When it comes to the realm of workplace romance, barriers are not only required but also essential for the development of tension, conflict, and eventually, a love narrative that is engaging and rewarding. These challenges may manifest themselves in a variety of configurations, both internal and external, and they operate as stimulants for the growth and development of one's character. Increasing the stakes, intensifying the emotional journey, and keeping readers hooked until the very end are all things that may be accomplished by deliberately inserting difficulties into your workplace romance story.

When it comes to the characters, internal hurdles are firmly ingrained inside themselves. These difficulties often originate from the characters' previous experiences, anxieties, or personal issues. The protagonists are forced to confront their anxieties, face their weaknesses, and eventually develop as persons as a result of these challenges, which brings an additional layer of depth to the relationship. Take, for instance, the possibility that one of your major characters has been damaged in a past relationship at work, which has caused them to be reluctant about venturing into a new romantic engagement. Creating a captivating narrative arc that highlights the protagonist's personal development and the victory of love may be accomplished by enabling them to conquer their anxieties and by investigating the traumatic experiences they have had in the past.

On the other hand, external impediments are factors that come from the outside and function as a barrier to the romantic relationship between the characters. These impediments might take the form of anything from professional disagreements and rivalries to social expectations and misconceptions within the individual. One example would be if your main character and the person you are romantically involved with were competing for the same promotion at work. They are forced to manage the delicate balance between their professional aspirations and their increasing affections for one other as a result of the rivalry, which produces tension and struggle throughout the relationship. You are able to elevate the stakes, establish a feeling of urgency, and generate an emotional involvement for the readers by skillfully using this external hurdle.

One thing that should be kept in mind is that impediments should not be employed for the sole purpose of causing conflict without any other reason. They should have a function in the narrative, leading to the development of the character and providing a layer of complexity to the romantic relationship. It is important to choose each barrier with great care and include it into the story that you are telling in order to make it seem natural and credible. Because of this, you will be able to write a workplace romance that is not only captivating and interesting but also keeps the readers on the edge of their seats.

To effectively use obstacles, consider the following:

A. **Relevance**: Ensure that the obstacles you introduce are relevant to the workplace environment and the characters' personal journeys. They should align with the overarching themes and conflicts of the story.

B. **Gradual Intensification**: Start with smaller obstacles and gradually increase their complexity and impact. This allows for a natural progression of tension and keeps readers engaged throughout the story.

C. **Character Development**: Use obstacles as opportunities for character development. Allow your characters to face challenges, make difficult choices, and grow as individuals. This not only adds depth to their personalities but also strengthens the emotional connection between them and the readers.

D. **Resolution and Growth**: Ultimately, the obstacles should lead to a resolution that feels satisfying and authentic. Whether the characters overcome the obstacles together or individually, the resolution should showcase their growth, resilience, and the strength of their love.

Adding some challenges to your workplace romance novel can really make the story more engaging and emotionally impactful for your readers. These challenges, both within and outside ourselves, really push us to grow, create some tension, and in the end, lead to a love story that lasts through it all.

5

THE POWER OF CONVERSATION: EXPLORING DIALOGUE AND INTERACTION

Writing Engaging and Realistic Dialogue

Dialogue is a strong element that may be used in workplace romance novels to bring the characters to life and carry the tale along. Readers are more likely to have a stronger connection to the characters and the connections between them when they perceive authentic and engaging language. In this part, we will discuss the skill of developing conversation that is both natural and interesting, with the goal of ensuring that your workplace romance book connects with readers.

To get started, finding a balance between the three elements of description, action, and communication is essential. Although communication is essential to every scene, depending only on chats might result in a monotonous experience for the protagonist. Your ability to produce a dynamic story that interests readers directly correlates to your ability to interweave conversation with action and descriptive details. For instance, rather than having people participate in a long speech exchange, you may want to think about adding their motions, gestures, and facial expressions into the scenario to improve its visual attractiveness. Not only does this give the characters more dimension, but it also makes it possible for the conversation to flow naturally within the larger framework of the plot because of this.

In addition, the use of dialogue tags and actions may assist in the communication of feelings and the maintenance of the reader's attention. Instead of only describing the conversation, you may want to consider incorporating tags indicating how the words are uttered. The phrases "she whispered" and "he exclaimed" are two examples that may give insights into the characters' emotional states, adding depth and authenticity to the interactions between them. As an additional point of interest, incorporating actions between lines of language may break up the discussion and provide a more realistic rhythm. For instance, a character may stop, take a sip of coffee, or anxiously fidget with their pen. This would let the reader imagine the situation and completely immerse themselves in the moment.

For the purpose of demonstration, let us look at an example. Imagine Emily and Alex, two coworkers, developing a budding romantic relationship in the workplace. You could want to bring a little bit of fun and playfulness into the talk rather than having a simple chat about how they feel about one another.

For example, Emily may be seen smiling cheekily. "So, Alex, are you going to tell me you've been moonlighting as a secret agent all this time?" While reclining back in his chair, Alex giggles. "If I were, I wouldn't be able to share classified information with you, now would I?"

You can create a more interesting and memorable relationship between the characters by including humor and light banter in the discourse. This gives their connection more depth and keeps readers anxiously turning the pages of the book.

When it comes to writing a great workplace romance book, having realistic and interesting dialogue is necessary. Through the use of dialogue, action, and description, the incorporation of dialogue tags and actions, and the incorporation of humor and authenticity into conversations, you can create captivating interactions that grab readers and bring your characters to life. Use the power of conversation and allow it to serve as the primary motivating factor behind the emotional connection between your characters and the people who read your work.

SETTING HEALTHY BOUNDARIES IN THE WORKPLACE

Building Relatable Protagonists

To create relatable protagonists in a workplace romance novel, it is crucial to delve into their backgrounds, motivations, and internal conflicts. By understanding these key aspects of your characters, you can develop their personalities in a way that resonates with readers, making them feel real and human.

Start by exploring the protagonists' past experiences and how they have shaped their present selves. Consider their upbringing, education, and previous work experiences. These factors can influence their beliefs, values, and perspectives, providing a foundation for their actions and decisions throughout the story.

In addition to their backgrounds, it is essential to showcase the vulnerabilities of your protagonists. No one is perfect, and by revealing their flaws and insecurities, you create multidimensional characters that readers can empathize with. Whether it's a fear of failure, a struggle with self-doubt, or a past heartbreak, these vulnerabilities add depth and relatability to your protagonists.

Furthermore, highlight the strengths of your protagonists. These strengths can be both professional and personal, showcasing their expertise in the workplace and their admirable qualities as individuals. By showcasing their strengths alongside their vulnerabilities, you create a balanced portrayal that reflects the complexities of real people.

To make your protagonists relatable on a personal level, tap into universally understood experiences and emotions. Whether it's the joy of achieving a long-awaited promotion, the frustration of dealing with a difficult coworker, or the fear of taking a risk in love, these emotions resonate with readers and create a connection between them and your characters.

By building relatable protagonists, you lay the foundation for a compelling workplace romance. Readers will become invested in their journey, rooting for them to overcome obstacles and find love amidst the challenges of the workplace.

For example, in the workplace romance novel *"A Second Chance at Love,"* the protagonist, Emma, is a hardworking and ambitious marketing executive who is haunted by a past failure. Through flashbacks and introspective moments, readers learn about Emma's struggles with self-doubt and fear of repeating past mistakes. As the story progresses, Emma's vulnerability and determination to succeed resonate with readers who have faced similar challenges in their own careers. This relatability creates an emotional connection, making readers eager to see Emma find not only professional success but also a fulfilling romantic relationship.

By focusing on building relatable protagonists, you ensure that your workplace romance novel resonates with readers on an emotional level. Through their strengths, vulnerabilities, and shared experiences, your protagonists become characters that readers can root for and relate to, creating a compelling and engaging story.

Designing Dynamic Love Interests

To create dynamic love interests for your workplace romance novel, it is essential to strike a balance between their strengths and flaws. While it may be tempting to create perfect characters, it is the flaws that add depth and make them more relatable to readers. By showing how their strengths complement the weaknesses of the protagonist and vice versa, you can create a dynamic and engaging relationship that drives the romantic tension and conflicts throughout the story.

When designing your love interests, consider their individual arcs and how they intertwine with the main plot. Just like the protagonists, the love interests should have their own goals, motivations, and conflicts that add layers to the story. By giving them their own journey, you can create a more complex and compelling relationship that keeps readers invested.

To make your love interests as realistic as possible, delve into their backgrounds and experiences. What events in their past have shaped them into the people they are today? How do these experiences influence their actions and decisions within the workplace? By understanding their history, you can develop well-rounded characters that readers can connect with on a deeper level.

In addition to their individual traits, it is important to consider how the love interests interact with the workplace environment. How do their roles within the company affect their relationship with the protagonist? Are there any conflicts of interest or power dynamics that add tension to their romance? Exploring these dynamics allows you to create a workplace romance that feels authentic and grounded in reality.

Remember, the key to designing dynamic love interests is to make them as complex and multidimensional as the protagonists themselves. By giving them strengths, flaws, and their own personal journeys, you can create a relationship that captivates readers and keeps them turning the pages.

Creating Memorable Supporting Characters

In every workplace romance novel, the supporting characters play a crucial role in enriching the story and supporting the development of the protagonists and love interests. These characters add depth to the world of the story and create a more immersive reading experience. To create memorable supporting characters, it is important to give each one a clear purpose and unique personality traits that differentiate them from one another.

One way to create memorable supporting characters is by ensuring that they serve a specific function in the narrative. Whether it's providing comedic relief, offering guidance, or posing challenges to the main characters, each supporting character should have a role that contributes to the overall story. For example, in a workplace romance set in a law firm, you could have a quirky paralegal who brings humor and levity to the office environment, a wise mentor who provides guidance to the protagonist, or a rival colleague who creates tension and competition.

Another key aspect of creating memorable supporting characters is giving them distinct personality traits. Each character should have their own unique voice, mannerisms, and quirks that make them stand out. This could be reflected in their dialogue, actions, or even their physical appearance. For instance, you could have a supporting character who always wears colorful socks, speaks in a distinct accent, or has a habit of quoting Shakespeare during meetings. These small details can make the character more memorable and add depth to their portrayal.

Furthermore, it is important to ensure that the supporting characters have their own arcs that intertwine with the main plot. Just like the protagonists and love interests, the supporting characters should experience growth and change throughout the story. This could involve facing their own challenges, overcoming personal obstacles, or learning important life lessons. By giving the supporting characters their own journeys, you create a more dynamic and engaging narrative that keeps readers invested in the story as a whole.

To illustrate the importance of memorable supporting characters, let's consider the workplace romance novel "Love in the Office." In this story, the protagonist, Sarah, works in a bustling advertising agency. Alongside her, there is a supporting character named Lily, who is a free-spirited graphic designer with a penchant for unconventional ideas. Lily's purpose in the narrative is to provide comedic relief and challenge Sarah's more traditional approach to work. Her unique personality traits, such as her vibrant fashion sense and love for street art, make her a memorable character that readers will fondly remember.

Creating memorable supporting characters is essential in crafting a compelling workplace romance novel. By giving each character a clear purpose, distinct personality traits, and their own arcs, you add depth and richness to the story. These characters serve as a catalyst for the development of the protagonists and love interests, offering guidance, posing challenges, and providing comedic relief. Through their presence, the world of the story becomes more immersive, creating a reading experience that captivates and resonates with readers.

7

LAUGHTER IN THE PAGES

Crafting witty banter and playful interactions between characters is a crucial aspect of incorporating humor into a workplace romance novel. These moments not only entertain readers but also reveal character traits and deepen relationships. By using techniques such as wordplay, sarcasm, and banter, authors can create engaging and dynamic interactions that add depth to the romantic storyline.

One effective way to infuse humor into dialogue is through wordplay. Playing with language and using clever puns or double entendres can create moments of levity and amusement. For example, in a scene where the protagonist and love interest are discussing a project at work, the protagonist could make a witty comment that elicits a playful response from the love interest. This exchange showcases their chemistry and adds a touch of humor to the conversation.

Sarcasm can also be a powerful tool in creating humorous interactions. Characters with a sarcastic sense of humor can engage in witty banter, using irony and clever comebacks to keep readers entertained. This can be particularly effective in workplace settings where characters may use sarcasm to cope or navigate challenging situations. By infusing sarcasm into conversations, authors can add a layer of complexity to their characters and create moments of comedic relief.

Banter, characterized by playful and lighthearted exchanges, is another technique to incorporate humor into workplace romance novels. This type of interaction often involves quick-witted remarks and teasing between characters. For instance, during a casual lunch break, the protagonist and their coworker could engage in banter about a funny incident that happened at work. This banter not only showcases their camaraderie but also adds a light-hearted touch to the story.

It is essential to remember that while humor is a vital element in workplace romance novels, it should be balanced with the serious plots and emotional depth of the story. The integration of humor should enhance the overall narrative rather than undermine the serious themes. By juxtaposing light moments with intense or dramatic scenes, authors can create a well-rounded story that resonates with readers on multiple levels. Humor should enrich the emotional journey of the characters and contribute to the impact of the romantic storyline.

Writing witty banter and playful interactions between characters is an effective way to incorporate humor into a workplace romance novel. Authors can create engaging and dynamic dialogues that reveal character traits and deepen relationships by utilizing wordplay, sarcasm, and banter. However, it is crucial to maintain a balance between humor and serious plots, ensuring that the comedic moments enhance the overall narrative and contribute to the story's emotional depth.

8

"MASTERING THE ART OF CLIMAX AND RESOLUTION"

Building to an Emotionally Satisfying Climax

To create an emotionally satisfying climax for your workplace romance novel, it is crucial to carefully build tension and raise the stakes throughout the narrative. By gradually intensifying both the romantic and workplace conflicts, you can captivate readers and keep them invested in the outcome of the story.

Begin by exploring the growth and evolution of your main characters as they navigate these challenges. Show how they confront their fears, face their flaws, and learn from their mistakes. By highlighting their personal development, you can create a sense of anticipation and emotional investment in their journey.

As the story progresses, escalate the tension between the protagonists, both in their romantic relationship and in their professional lives. Introduce obstacles and complications that test the strength of their bond and force them to confront difficult choices. This can include conflicts arising from workplace dynamics, ethical dilemmas, or external pressures that threaten to tear them apart.

Consider the pacing of your narrative. Gradually increase the pace as the climax approaches, creating a sense of urgency and heightened emotions. This can be achieved through shorter, more intense scenes, as well as by increasing the frequency and intensity of the conflicts faced by the characters.

Ultimately, the emotionally satisfying climax should resolve the central tension of the story in a compelling and cathartic way. It should feel earned and resonate with readers on an emotional level. Consider the impact of the resolution on both the romantic relationship and the characters' professional lives. By addressing both aspects, you can create a climax that feels complete and satisfying.

To illustrate this, let's consider an example. Imagine a workplace romance between a high-powered CEO and a talented but overlooked employee. Throughout the story, their relationship is tested by power struggles, office politics, and conflicting priorities. As the climax approaches, the CEO must make a difficult decision that could either save the company or risk losing the employee they have come to love. The tension builds as the characters face the consequences of their choices, leading to a climactic moment where they must confront their fears and make a final, life-changing decision. This emotionally charged climax not only resolves the romantic conflict but also addresses the professional challenges they have faced, providing a satisfying conclusion to the story.

By carefully building tension and resolving conflicts in a way that feels authentic and emotionally resonant, you can create an emotionally satisfying climax that will leave readers captivated and fulfilled.

Resolving Workplace and Romantic Conflicts

To create a satisfying resolution in a workplace romance novel, it is essential to address and resolve the workplace and romantic conflicts that have been building throughout the story. By authenticating these conflicts, the narrative can reach a conclusion that feels earned and resonates with readers.

When resolving workplace conflicts, it is important to showcase the characters' growth and evolution as they navigate the complexities of their relationships within the professional environment. This includes addressing power dynamics, ethical concerns, and the consequences of their actions. By delving into these issues, the story can provide a realistic portrayal of the challenges faced by individuals involved in workplace romances.

For example, if the main characters are colleagues who have fallen in love, they may need to confront the potential consequences of their relationship on their careers. This conflict could be resolved by having the characters openly communicate with their superiors or HR department, demonstrating their commitment to maintaining profession-alism and ensuring that their personal lives do not interfere with their work responsibilities. By addressing this work-place conflict head-on, the characters can find a way to navigate the challenges and continue their romance in a way that is acceptable within the professional setting.

In addition to resolving workplace conflicts, it is equally important to address the romantic conflicts that have arisen between the main characters. These conflicts may stem from misunderstandings, past traumas, or external obstacles that have tested their relationship throughout the story. By authentically resolving these conflicts, the story can provide a sense of closure and satisfaction to the readers.

For instance, if the main characters have been struggling with trust issues due to past heartbreaks, the resolution could involve a heartfelt conversation where they openly express their fears and insecurities. By allowing the charac-ters to confront their emotional barriers and work through them together, the story can demonstrate their growth and commitment to each other. This resolution not only provides a satisfying conclusion to the romantic conflict but also reinforces the emotional connection between the characters, leaving readers with a sense of hope and fulfillment.

By effectively resolving both workplace and romantic conflicts, the workplace romance novel can reach a conclusion that feels emotionally satisfying and resonates with readers. It is through the resolution of these conflicts that the characters can find closure, growth, and ultimately, a happily ever after.

Delivering a Memorable and Fulfilling Resolution

Crafting a memorable resolution is essential in leaving a lasting impact on readers and providing a sense of closure and satisfaction to the workplace romance narrative. In this section, we will explore the essential elements of a fulfilling resolution that aligns with the themes and character journeys established throughout the book.

To deliver a memorable resolution, it is crucial to tie up all loose ends and complete the character arcs in a way that feels emotionally satisfying. Readers invest their time and emotions in the story, and they deserve a resolution that resonates with them. Here are some strategies to consider:

Closure: Provide a sense of closure by addressing all the major storylines and plot points. Ensure that the conflicts, both professional and personal, are resolved in a way that feels authentic and meaningful. Give readers a clear understanding of how the characters have grown and changed throughout the narrative.

For example, if the workplace romance involves a power imbalance between the characters, the resolution could involve a shift in the dynamics, where both individuals find a more equal footing. This closure allows readers to see the characters' journey come full circle and provides a satisfying conclusion to their story.

Reflection: Incorporate moments of reflection where the characters reflect on their experiences and the lessons they have learned. This allows readers to see the main characters' growth and development and reinforces the themes explored in the workplace romance novel.

For instance, if one of the characters struggles with maintaining a work-life balance, the resolution could include a moment of reflection where they realize the importance of prioritizing their personal life and making time for their relationships. This reflection adds depth to the resolution and allows readers to connect with the characters on a deeper level.

Hope for the Future: End the workplace romance novel with a sense of hope for the future. Show readers that the characters have overcome their challenges and are now moving forward with a renewed sense of purpose and optimism. This hopeful note leaves readers with a positive and uplifting feeling, ensuring they remember the story long after they have finished reading.

For example, the resolution could include a glimpse into the characters' lives after the workplace romance, where they have found success in their careers and are now in a healthy and fulfilling relationship. This glimpse into the future provides a sense of closure while also leaving room for readers to imagine the characters' continued happiness.

Crafting a memorable and fulfilling resolution requires careful consideration of the story's themes, character arcs, and reader expectations. By providing closure, reflection, and hope for the future, you can create a resolution that resonates with readers and leaves a lasting impression.

9

POLISHING THE PROSE: EDITING AND REFINING THE MANUSCRIPT

Editing and Refining the Manuscript

Editing is a crucial step in the writing process that ensures your workplace romance novel is clear, coherent, and engaging for readers. In this section, we will explore the importance of editing for clarity and consistency, providing you with valuable tips to refine your manuscript.

Emphasizing Clarity

One of the primary goals of editing is to ensure that your storyline is coherent and easy to follow. As a workplace romance author, it is essential to guide your readers through the intricacies of the romance while maintaining clarity. To achieve this, consider the following:

- Review the flow of your plot: Examine the sequence of events and transitions between scenes. Ensure that each scene contributes to the narrative and moves the story forward.
- Eliminate ambiguity: Pay attention to any confusing or unclear passages. Clarify your characters' intentions, motivations, and emotions to avoid leaving readers puzzled.
- Streamline your prose: Simplify complex sentences and eliminate unnecessary jargon. Aim for concise, straightforward language that immerses readers in the story.

Maintaining Consistency

Consistency is key to creating a seamless reading experience for your audience. By maintaining consistency in character traits, plot points, and overall narrative flow, you can ensure that readers remain engaged throughout your workplace romance novel. Consider the following tips:

- Character consistency: Review your characters' traits, behaviors, and motivations to ensure they remain consistent throughout the story. Make sure their actions align with their established personalities, avoiding any sudden or unexplained changes.

- Plot consistency: Examine the progression of your plot and ensure that it remains logical and coherent. Check for any plot holes or inconsistencies that may disrupt the readers' immersion in the story.
- Narrative flow: Pay attention to the pacing of your workplace romance novel. Ensure that each chapter and scene flows smoothly into the next, creating a cohesive narrative that keeps readers captivated.

Polishing Dialogue for Clarity

Dialogue is vital in workplace romance novels, as it reveals character traits, advances the story, and builds emotional connections between characters. When editing your manuscript, focus on polishing dialogue to enhance its clarity and impact. Consider the following techniques:

- Eliminate ambiguity: Review your dialogue exchanges and ensure the intentions and emotions behind each character's words are clear. Avoid vague or cryptic dialogue that may confuse readers.
- Enhance character interactions: Pay attention to the dynamics between characters in your workplace romance. Ensure that the dialogue reflects their relationships, whether it be romantic tension, professional conflicts, or supportive camaraderie.
- Use dialogue tags and actions strategically: Break up dialogue with descriptive tags and actions to add

variety and maintain reader engagement. This will also help readers visualize the characters' movements and expressions during conversations.

Editing your workplace romance novel for clarity and consistency can elevate the quality of your storytelling. Remember to focus on creating a clear and engaging narrative flow, maintaining consistency in character traits and plot progression, and polishing dialogue to enhance its impact. With these editing techniques, your manuscript will captivate readers and leave them eagerly turning the pages.

10

HARNESSING INNER DRIVE: STAYING MOTIVATED AS A WRITER

Overcoming Writer's Block

Writer's block can be a frustrating and discouraging experience, but there are strategies you can employ to overcome it and keep your creativity flowing. In this section, we will explore various techniques that can help you break through mental blocks and reignite your writing inspiration.

One effective method for combating writer's block is to take breaks and change your environment. Sometimes, stepping away from your writing for a short period can provide the mental clarity you need. Take a walk, engage in a physical activity, or simply relax and clear your mind. By giving yourself permission to take a break, you allow your subconscious to continue working on your story in the background, often leading to fresh ideas and renewed motivation when you return to your writing.

Another helpful technique is freewriting. Set a timer for a specific amount of time, such as ten minutes, and write without any constraints or expectations. Don't worry about grammar, punctuation, or even coherence. The goal is to let your thoughts flow freely onto the page without judgment. This exercise can help you bypass your inner critic and tap into your creativity, allowing new ideas to emerge.

Outlining, brainstorming, and mind mapping are additional strategies that can stimulate your creativity and help you overcome creative stagnation. By visually organizing your thoughts and ideas, you can identify new connections and possibilities within your story. Consider creating character profiles, plotting diagrams, or even visual collages to spark inspiration and generate fresh perspectives.

Engaging in activities that stimulate your senses and expose you to new experiences can also break through mental blocks. Read widely across different genres and authors, watch movies or TV shows outside of your usual preferences, visit museums or art galleries, or simply explore new places. These experiences can provide a fresh perspective, inspire new ideas, and infuse your writing with a renewed sense of excitement.

Remember, writer's block is a common challenge that many authors face. Don't be too hard on yourself when it happens. Instead, embrace these strategies and allow yourself the time and space to overcome it. By implementing these techniques and finding what works best for you, you can break free from writer's block and continue creating your compelling workplace romance novel.

Staying Motivated as a Writer

Setting Realistic Writing Goals

Setting realistic writing goals is crucial for maintaining focus and productivity as a writer. Breaking down larger writing projects into smaller, manageable tasks increases motivation and allows for more effective progress tracking. In this section, we will explore strategies for setting SMART goals and provide tips on reviewing and adjusting these goals to ensure continued growth as a writer.

Setting specific, measurable, achievable, relevant, and time-bound (**SMART**) goals is the foundation of effective goal-setting. When goals are specific, it becomes easier to outline the steps needed to achieve them. For example, instead of setting a vague goal like "finish writing a novel," a specific goal could be "write 1,000 words per day for the next three months." This specific goal provides clarity and helps writers stay on track.

Measurable goals allow for progress tracking and provide a sense of accomplishment. For instance, writers can set a goal to complete a certain number of chapters or reach a specific word count by a certain date. By measuring progress, writers can celebrate milestones along the way, further motivating them to continue writing.

Achievable goals are those that are within reach and can be accomplished with the available resources and time. It is important to be realistic about writing capabilities and the time that can be devoted to the craft. Setting goals that are too ambitious may lead to frustration and burnout. By setting achievable goals, writers can maintain a steady pace and sustain their motivation.

Relevant goals are those that align with overall writing aspirations. Writers should consider what they want to achieve and how each goal contributes to that vision. For example, if the ultimate goal is to publish a workplace romance novel, setting goals related to character development, plot structure, and dialogue writing would be relevant to the overall objective.

Time-bound goals have a specific deadline or timeframe attached to them. By setting deadlines, writers create a sense of urgency and prioritize their writing. For instance, a goal could be to complete the first draft of a novel within six months or to revise and polish a manuscript within a specific timeframe. A timeline helps writers stay accountable and focused on their writing goals.

Regularly reviewing and adjusting writing goals is essential for maintaining motivation and growth as a writer. As writers progress in their writing journey, they may find that certain goals must be modified or replaced. By regularly evaluating goals, writers can ensure they remain relevant and aligned with their evolving writing aspirations. Seeking feedback from trusted peers or mentors can provide fresh perspectives and insights that inform the goal-setting process.

Remember, setting realistic writing goals is not about putting unnecessary pressure on oneself, but rather about maintaining a sense of direction and purpose in the writing journey. By setting SMART goals, reviewing and adjusting them as needed, writers can stay motivated and steadily progress towards achieving their writing dreams.

Finding Inspiration and Support

Finding inspiration and seeking support are crucial aspects of staying motivated as a writer. In this section, we will explore various strategies to ignite your creativity and connect with a community of fellow writers who can provide encouragement, feedback, and accountability.

Seeking Inspiration from Various Sources

To keep your writing fresh and vibrant, it's essential to draw inspiration from a wide range of sources. Real-life events, personal experiences, and other narratives can serve as well-springs of creativity. Take the time to observe the world around you, engage in meaningful conversations, and reflect on your own emotions and experiences. These elements can enrich your storytelling and infuse your workplace romance novel with authenticity.

For example, if your workplace romance is set in a hospital, you might draw inspiration from the challenges and triumphs of healthcare professionals. By immersing yourself in their world, you can capture the nuances of their daily lives and create relatable characters and situations.

Joining Writing Groups and Workshops

Connecting with other writers who share your passion can provide invaluable support and inspiration. Consider joining a writing group or attending workshops where you can interact with like-minded individuals. These communities offer a platform to exchange ideas, receive constructive feedback, and learn from one another's experiences.

In these settings, you can discuss your workplace romance novel with fellow writers who understand the genre's unique challenges. They can offer fresh perspectives, identify areas for improvement, and provide encouragement during moments of self-doubt. Additionally, participating in writing exercises and workshops can help you refine your skills and explore new techniques to enhance your story-telling.

Engaging in Continuing Education

As a writer, it's important to expand your knowledge and skills constantly. Continuing education can provide opportunities to explore new genres, techniques, and writing styles. Consider taking writing classes or attending seminars to deepen your understanding of storytelling principles and refine your craft.

Reading widely across different genres and styles can inspire fresh ideas and broaden your creative horizons. Immersing yourself in diverse narratives can help you gain insights into effective storytelling techniques and discover unique approaches to workplace romance. Don't be afraid to venture outside your comfort zone and explore new literary territories.

Exploring Online Writing Communities

In the digital age, online writing communities offer a convenient and accessible way to connect with fellow writers. Platforms such as writing forums, social media groups, and online critique circles allow you to share your work, receive feedback, and discuss various writing-related topics.

These communities provide a supportive environment where you can find encouragement, motivation, and accountability. By actively participating in these online spaces, you can forge connections with writers worldwide, exchange ideas, and gain valuable insights into the craft of writing workplace romance novels.

Remember, finding inspiration and support is an ongoing process. Stay open to new experiences, seek out diverse perspectives, and remain engaged with the writing community. By nurturing these connections and continuously seeking inspiration, you can overcome challenges, stay motivated, and create a workplace romance novel that resonates with readers.

11

TYING THE KNOT OF LOVE IN THE WORKPLACE

Crafting an Epilogue that Resonates

Writing an epilogue that hits home is super important for wrapping up your workplace romance novel. The epilogue wraps things up, giving readers a peek into what happens to the characters after everything has settled down. It's a chance to wrap things up, give some finality to character stories, and make a memorable impression on your readers.

To wrap things up nicely, it's important to go back to some of the main themes or motifs from your novel. Consider the key elements that have played a big role in the story and find a way to weave them into the epilogue. This will keep things flowing and remind readers of the adventure they've shared with your characters.

Besides going back to those themes, think about how your main characters have grown and changed. Highlight how they've changed from the start of the story, both as individuals and together. You can totally see this through what they think, how they act, or what they say. Showing how they've grown lets readers see the effects of their workplace romance and the changes it has caused.

When writing the epilogue, it's key to find that sweet spot between giving a sense of closure and leaving some space for readers to think about what might happen next. Help them feel good by sorting out any leftover issues or questions they might have. But hey, don't feel like you have to wrap everything up perfectly. Drop a little tease about what's to come without spilling all the beans, so readers can guess and picture what happens to the characters after your story wraps up.

Think about how each resolution feels in the epilogue. Try to wrap things up in a way that fits the vibe of your workplace romance. No matter if it's a mix of happy and sad vibes, a fun party, or a deep moment of thought, just make sure the feelings match up with what your characters have been through.

Writing an epilogue that really hits home takes some thought and a bit of planning. This is your last chance to really make an impression on your readers. If you take a look back at the main themes, wrap up the storylines, and hit the right emotional notes, you can whip up an epilogue that really enhances your workplace romance novel and sticks with readers who've followed your characters' adventures.

Next up, we'll dive into how to wrap up storylines to give the narrative some nice closure and satisfaction.

Finalizing Storylines

Writing a workplace romance novel means making sure all the storylines wrap up nicely and that every character's journey feels complete. Wrapping up storylines is super important for giving readers that satisfying feeling, making sure they walk away happy. In this part, we'll dive into how to wrap up storylines and chat about some cool ways to craft memorable endings.

First off, it's super important to map out how each character's journey wraps up. Think about the feelings you want to bring out and how they fit with the vibe of your workplace romance story. Consider how your main characters grow and change, and how their journeys can wrap up nicely. Think about the challenges they dealt with in the story and make sure their solutions show how they tackled those hurdles.

While wrapping up your storylines, just keep an eye on how the pacing flows in your narrative. Try to give each character a proper wrap-up at the right times, steering clear of any hasty or sudden endings. Think about what each resolution means and how it ties into the bigger themes and messages of your novel. If you give each storyline the attention it needs, you can wrap things up in a way that feels connected and meaningful.

Also, think about how your resolutions affect your readers. Consider the questions they might have had during the story and make sure to answer them well. Wrap up any loose ends and clear up any unresolved issues. This will give your readers a nice wrap-up and help them fully get what's going on with the workplace romance you've created.

Let's take a look at why wrapping up storylines is super important with a quick example. In a workplace romance story set in a corporate office, our main character, Sarah, is caught between her career goals and her budding feelings for her coworker, Mark. In the story, Sarah deals with some personal struggles and outside challenges that really put her dedication to her job and her relationship with Mark to the test. As the story goes on, Sarah has to make a decision that will shape her future.

In the last chapters, it's super important to wrap things up in a way that shows how much Sarah has grown and the decisions she's made. So, Sarah might choose to focus on her career and take a break from her relationship with Mark. She might have figured out that it's time to concentrate on her career goals right now. Wrapping up Sarah's storyline like this lets readers see her personal growth and get a feel for the struggles she dealt with while juggling her career and love life.

Wrapping up storylines is super important when you're putting together a workplace romance novel. If you take the time to plan out how each character's story wraps up, think about the feelings involved, and tackle what readers are curious about, you can come up with endings that really hit home and feel complete. Think about how your characters have grown and changed, making sure their endings fit with the main themes and messages of your story. Doing this will totally give your readers a feeling of satisfaction and a memorable vibe from your workplace romance story.

Celebrating Your Success

Writing a workplace romance novel means making sure all the storylines wrap up nicely and that every character's journey feels complete. Wrapping up storylines is super important for giving readers that satisfying feeling, making sure they walk away happy. In this part, we'll dive into how to wrap up storylines and chat about some cool ways to craft memorable endings.

First off, it's super important to map out how each character's journey wraps up. Think about the feelings you want to bring out and how they fit with the vibe of your workplace romance story. Consider how your main characters grow and change, and how their journeys can wrap up nicely.

Think about the challenges they dealt with in the story and make sure their solutions show how they tackled those hurdles.

When you're wrapping up your storylines, just keep an eye on how the pacing flows in your narrative. Try to give each character a proper wrap-up at the right times, steering clear of any hasty or sudden endings. Think about what each resolution means and how it ties into the bigger themes and messages of your novel. If you give each storyline the attention it needs, you can wrap things up in a way that feels connected and meaningful.

Also, think about how your resolutions affect your readers. Consider the questions they might have had during the story and make sure to answer them well. Wrap up any loose ends and clear up any unresolved issues. This will give your readers a nice wrap-up and help them fully get what's going on with the workplace romance you've created.

Let's take a look at why wrapping up storylines is super important with a quick example. In a workplace romance story set in a corporate office, our main character, Sarah, is caught between her career goals and her budding feelings for her coworker, Mark. In the story, Sarah deals with some personal struggles and outside challenges that really put her dedication to her job and her relationship with Mark to the test. As the story goes on, Sarah has to make a decision that will shape her future.

In the last chapters, it's super important to wrap things up in a way that shows how much Sarah has grown and the decisions she's made. So, Sarah might choose to focus on her career and take a break from her relationship with Mark. She might have figured out that it's time to concentrate on her career goals right now. Wrapping up Sarah's storyline like this lets readers see her personal growth and get a feel for the struggles she dealt with while juggling her career and love life.

Wrapping up storylines is super important when you're putting together a workplace romance novel. If you take the time to plan out how each character's story wraps up, think about the feelings involved, and tackle what readers are curious about, you can come up with endings that really hit home and feel complete. Think about how your characters have grown and changed, making sure their endings fit with the main themes and messages of your story. Doing this will totally give your readers a feeling of satisfaction and a memorable vibe from your workplace romance story.

Writing a workplace romance novel is definitely a challenge. It takes commitment, sticking with it, and really getting to know the genre. As you wrap up your writing journey, take a sec to celebrate what you've accomplished. Hey, just wanted to give a shoutout to all the hard work you put into bringing your story to life! Think about the hurdles you got past, the things you picked up along the way, and how you grew as a writer during this journey.

One cool way to celebrate your success is by showing off your work to others. Think about hitting up some beta readers or other writers who can give you some good feedback on your manuscript. Their thoughts and views can totally help you polish your story and make it even better. Take constructive criticism in stride and see it as a chance to level up your writing skills.

Another fun way to celebrate is by trying to get your workplace romance novel published. Check out some literary agents or publishing houses that focus on romance novels and send them your manuscript. Hey, just keep in mind that every successful author had to start from the beginning, even if the publishing process feels a bit overwhelming. Keep at it and trust in the strength of your story.

Besides showing off your work to others, make sure to take a moment to think about what you've achieved. Think about the hurdles you tackled, like figuring out how to create that romantic spark or dealing with the tricky stuff at work. Think about how much you've grown as a writer, from that very first word you typed to the last page you finished. Appreciate the effort and passion that went into creating your characters and their love story.

While you're enjoying your success, don't forget to feel good about what you've achieved. Let your friends, family, and fellow writers in on your achievements! Take a moment to enjoy the feeling of finishing that workplace romance novel, knowing you've made something pretty awesome.

Celebrating your wins is great, but it's just as crucial to use that energy to fuel your future writing projects. Use what you've picked up during this writing journey for your future projects. Try out some new goals, push yourself to dive into different genres or themes, and keep growing as a writer. Hey, just keep in mind that this is only the start of your writing adventure, and every win is a step toward even cooler things ahead.

Enjoying your wins is a key part of writing. Show off your work, look for ways to get it published, think about what you've achieved, and let that inspire you for what's next. Hey, just a reminder that writing a workplace romance novel is a big deal, and you should totally be proud of what you've accomplished. Enjoy the thrill of finishing a story, and let that vibe push you to keep writing awesome novels down the line.

www.ingramcontent.com/pod-product-compliance
Lightning Source LLC
Chambersburg PA
CBHW070512170726
48291CB00008B/2714